Enough is Enough

Jessica crossed her arms in front of her chest. "For your information, I do *not* want my car to be like Elizabeth's."

"Steven just wants to help you," Elizabeth said as she came in to the garage. "You should listen. He *is* older than you are."

"He's older than you, too," Jessica yelled. "And you don't let him tell you what to do. So stop bossing me around just because you're four minutes older. I'm sick of it. And I'm sick of you!"

Elizabeth's face turned red. "Shut up," she yelled back.

"I will not. It used to be fun having a twin sister," Jessica went on. "But it isn't fun anymore—it's a big pain."

Bantam Skylark Books in the SWEET VALLEY KIDS series

SWEET VALLEY KIDS

THE BIG RACE

Written by
Molly Mia Stewart

Created by
FRANCINE PASCAL

Illustrated by
Ying-Hwa Hu

A BANTAM SKYLARK BOOK®
NEW YORK · TORONTO · LONDON · SYDNEY · AUCKLAND

RL 2, 005–008

THE BIG RACE

A Bantam Skylark Book / March 1993

*Sweet Valley High® and Sweet Valley Kids are trademarks of
Francine Pascal*

Conceived by Francine Pascal

*Produced by Daniel Weiss Associates, Inc.
33 West 17th Street
New York, NY 10011*

Covert art by Susan Tang

*Skylark Books is a registered trademark of Bantam Books, a division
of Bantam Doubleday Dell Publishing Group, Inc.
Registered in
U.S. Patent and Trademark Office and elsewhere.*

ISBN 0-553-48011-1

Published simultaneously in the United States and Canada

*Bantam Books are published by Bantam Books, a division of Bantam
Doubleday Dell Publishing Group, Inc. Its trademark, consisting of the
words "Bantam Books" and the portrayal of a rooster, is Registered in
U.S. Patent and Trademark Office and in other countries. Marca
Registrada. Bantam Books, 666 Fifth Avenue, New York, New York
10103.*

PRINTED IN THE UNITED STATES OF AMERICA

CWO   0 9 8 7 6 5 4 3 2 1

To Amanda Lapka

CHAPTER 1

The Announcement

"Ricky Capaldo has a new brother," Jessica Wakefield told her family as she sat down at the breakfast table. "His name is Johnny."

Jessica's twin sister, Elizabeth, swallowed a bite of her cereal and nodded. "He was born at two thirty A.M."

"They'll have to have his birthday parties in the middle of the night," Jessica joked.

"We don't have *your* birthday parties in the middle of the night," Mr. Wakefield said to Jessica. "And you and Elizabeth were born after midnight. So was Steven." Steven was the twins' older brother.

"I didn't know that," Elizabeth said. "What time were we born?"

Mrs. Wakefield smiled. "You were born at one fifteen A.M. And Jessica was born exactly four minutes later, at one nineteen A.M."

Jessica and Elizabeth looked at each other. It made sense that one of them had been born first. But the twins had never thought about it before.

"Now I know why Elizabeth always does her chores and homework first," Steven said. "And why she's never late for the school bus, like Jessica is. Elizabeth acts more grown-up because she's older."

It was true that Elizabeth usually acted more responsibly than Jessica did. Even though they were identical twins, Elizabeth and Jessica were different from each other in many ways.

Elizabeth loved reading books, especially mystery stories and books about horses. She loved playing sports, especially soccer. In school, Elizabeth always paid attention to the teacher, and she always got good grades.

Jessica didn't read very much, but she enjoyed playing dress-up and she loved going to modern-dance class. She was good at sports, but she didn't play much because she didn't like to get her clothes dirty. Jessica thought that the best thing about school was passing notes and talking to her friends.

It was hard for some people to believe that Jessica and Elizabeth could be so different, especially since the twins looked exactly alike. Both girls had blue-green eyes and long blond hair with bangs. They shared a bedroom, and toys, and chores. Elizabeth

and Jessica both thought having a twin was fun. They were best friends.

Mr. Wakefield stood up and started carrying dishes to the sink. "I'd better go, or I'll be late to work."

Elizabeth jumped up, too. "Come on, Jessica. The bus will be here soon. We'd better not miss it."

"But I'm not finished eating," Jessica said, scooping a spoonful of cereal from her bowl.

Mrs. Wakefield looked at the kitchen clock. "You'd better listen to your big sister. You have to leave for the bus in three minutes—and you don't even have your shoes on yet."

Elizabeth grinned. "See, Jess? I told you." She liked hearing her mother call her Jessica's big sister.

When the twins got on the bus, Jessica took the window seat. Caroline Pearce was sitting right behind them. She had shoulder-length red hair. Neither Jessica nor Elizabeth liked Caroline much because she was a busybody and a tattletale.

Caroline leaned forward. "Jessica, you sat next to the window yesterday on the way home. You always take turns. So Elizabeth should be on the inside."

"Jessica can sit there," Elizabeth said. "I don't mind."

"Thanks, Liz," Jessica said happily.

Elizabeth thought it was only fair that Jessica should have the window seat. After all, Jessica *was* the baby of the family.

That morning in class, the twins' teacher, Mrs. Otis, made a special announcement.

"Sweet Valley Elementary School has decided to sponsor a soap-box derby," Mrs. Otis said. "It will be the first one held in Sweet Valley in ten years."

Eva Simpson, one of the twins' best friends, raised her hand. "What's a soap-box derby?"

"It's a kind of race," Mrs. Otis explained. "Each person who enters builds his or her own car out of wood, cardboard, metal scraps, plastic milk crates, and anything else you want to use. Soap-box cars don't have engines, though, so races are always downhill."

Mrs. Otis passed some old photographs of soap-box derbies around the classroom. Some of the photographs showed cars zipping across a finish line. In one, a boy was holding up a big trophy. Another showed a picture of a crash.

"This looks great," Kisho Murasaki said. "I'm definitely entering."

"Me, too," Jessica said. She turned to Elizabeth. "Isn't this exciting?"

Elizabeth nodded. She turned around to Todd Wilkins, who sat behind her. Todd played on the soccer team with Elizabeth. "Are you going to enter?"

"You bet," Todd said. "I'm going to be a race-car driver when I grow up. This will be my first competition."

"My car is going to go two thousand miles an hour," Elizabeth boasted.

Todd laughed. "If you go that fast, you'll win for sure."

"She will not," Ken Matthews spoke up. He sat next to Todd, and the two were very good friends. "Elizabeth can't win—because *I'm* going to!"

CHAPTER 2

Ken Brags

During recess, Jessica, Elizabeth, Todd, Eva, Ken, and Kisho pretended to drive race cars. Their racetrack was a huge chalk circle they'd drawn around the swing set. They ran around and around and around.

"Zoom," Elizabeth yelled, running as fast as she could.

"I'm passing you," Jessica called out, trying to catch up to her.

"No way," Elizabeth said. "I can go faster. I'm older, remember?"

Jessica stopped running and put her hands on her hips. "You can*not*," she yelled after Elizabeth. Then she turned to her friends Lila Fowler and Ellen Riteman, who were playing nearby on the swings. They weren't playing race cars because neither of them wanted to enter the derby. Jessica hoped they hadn't heard Elizabeth, but they had.

"I didn't know Elizabeth was older than you," Lila called out. "I thought you were twins."

"We *are* twins," Jessica said, stomping her foot. "Elizabeth is only four minutes older. It's not a big deal."

"It is too a big deal," Elizabeth said, running up in time to hear what Jessica was saying. Todd and Eva stopped right behind her. "It means Jessica is my little sister."

"Little sister?" Caroline asked. She was sitting on one of the swings. "Is that why you let Jessica sit by the window on the bus?"

"That's right," Elizabeth admitted. "I'm a *nice* big sister."

Jessica frowned. Caroline was a huge gossip. Jessica knew that in a few minutes, everyone in their class would know that Elizabeth was older. Jessica was also angry because Elizabeth was treating her like a little kid.

"You don't have to be nice to me at all," she told her sister.

"Don't complain, Jessica. I think you're the lucky one," Ellen said. "The youngest is always spoiled. My little brother, Mark, definitely is."

Jessica's face brightened. She gave Elizabeth a 'so there' look. Then she smiled at her friends. "If I'm spoiled, that means I get whatever I want—and I want to win the soap-box derby!"

"That won't happen," Elizabeth said. "You don't know anything about cars. At least I play with toy cars. My chances of winning are a lot better."

Just then, Ken and Kisho came running over from the chalk circle. "Hey, Jessica," Ken said. "Let's pretend we're driving in the Indy 500, and I win first place."

Jessica was glad Ken had changed the subject. "I have a better idea," she said. "Let's pretend you get a flat tire, and *I* win."

"That's stupid," Ken said. "I should win now, because I'm going to win for real. My dad was a soap-box champion. When he was a little older than me, he went all the way to Akron, Ohio, for the national finals."

"That's right," Todd said. "I've seen a photograph in your den of your dad with his trophy."

"Right," Ken said. "And my dad is going to help me build a car. It'll be the fastest one in the derby. The rest of you will eat my dust."

"Don't be so sure," Elizabeth said, sounding angry. "You're going to have tons of competition."

"That's right," Kisho said. "Our cars will be just as good."

"Yeah," Eva added. "Just wait."

"And maybe you'll eat *my* dust," Jessica said. She'd had enough of Ken's bragging. But Ken wasn't the only one bothering her.

"I'm going to win the derby," Jessica whispered to Lila and Ellen. "That'll show Ken—and Elizabeth, too."

CHAPTER 3

Tools and Supplies

"Mrs. Otis says we have to wear helmets," Elizabeth said, reaching for a cookie.

It was after school that day. Elizabeth, Jessica, and Steven had just told their mother all about the soap-box derby. She was almost as excited as they were.

"That's a very good idea," Mrs. Wakefield said. "We'll have to buy three, one for each of you."

"You only have to buy two helmets," Steven said.

"Aren't you entering?" Mrs. Wakefield asked.

"No," Steven said. "Soap-box derbies are for little kids."

"But this is your first chance to be in one," Mrs. Wakefield pointed out. "I'm sure it'll be a lot of fun."

Steven shook his head. "I'm too old."

Mrs. Wakefield shrugged and turned to the twins. "You two only have a week to build your cars," she reminded them. "We'd better do some shopping right away. Let's go to the mall as soon as you've finished your snack."

"I'm finished," Elizabeth said.

"Me, too," Jessica said.

"Yeah, let's go." Steven popped one last cookie in his mouth and headed for the back door. "I'm not entering, but I'll make sure Elizabeth and Jessica build their cars the right way. It's my job as their big brother."

Mrs. Wakefield laughed, while Elizabeth and Jessica rolled their eyes.

Fifteen minutes later, the Wakefields were in the lumber store buying wood. Then they walked next door to the hardware store and bought metal poles to hold the wheels of their cars. Once the twins attached wheels to the poles, the poles would be called "axles." Next the twins picked out plastic helmets at the bicycle shop. Then the Wakefields walked back to the car.

"Well, that's enough for one day," Mrs. Wakefield said as she unlocked the trunk.

"But we still don't have any wheels," Elizabeth said. She helped Mrs. Wakefield put their purchases in the trunk.

"And without wheels, we can't race," Jessica added.

Mrs. Wakefield nodded. "I was surprised the hardware store didn't sell any. But don't worry. We'll find some tomorrow."

Steven pointed across the parking lot. "Here come Mr. Matthews and Ken."

Ken was pulling a wagon packed with supplies. Mr. Matthews was carrying a large, stuffed paper bag. They walked toward the Wakefields.

"Hello, Colin," Mrs. Wakefield called out. Colin was Mr. Matthews's first name. "It's nice to see you."

"Hi there, Alice," Mr. Matthews said. Alice was Mrs. Wakefield's first name. "How are your classes going?" Mrs. Wakefield was learning to be an interior designer. She took classes at Sweet Valley University.

While the adults were talking, Jessica turned to Ken. "Did you find any wheels?"

"Yeah. I got great wheels," Ken said. "They're at the bottom of the wagon."

"Really?" Elizabeth said. "Where did you get them?"

"Why should I tell you?" Ken asked.

"Why *shouldn't* you tell us?" Jessica shot back.

"Ken must be afraid you two are going to beat him," Steven said.

"I am not," Ken protested. "I'm just not giving away any secrets." He tugged at his father's sleeve. "Can we go, Dad? I really want to start building the car."

Mrs. Wakefield looked at her watch. "It is getting late. We'd better get home as well. Bye Colin, bye Ken."

Elizabeth was glad to go. Usually Ken was nice, but Elizabeth thought he had been acting obnoxious ever since Mrs. Otis had told them about the derby.

After dinner, Mr. Wakefield helped the twins clear out a space in the garage where they could work on their cars. Steven hung around, watching.

Mr. Wakefield got out hammers, screwdrivers, and pliers. He poured out little piles of nails and screws, and dug up pieces of sandpaper and cans of paint.

"You two are ready to start building," Mr. Wakefield announced. "I'll be back out in a little while to see how you're doing. Steven, I'm counting on you to make sure your sisters use the tools safely and properly."

"OK. And I'll make sure they put everything together just like the man at the hardware store told us," Steven said, as Mr. Wakefield went back into the house.

20

"This will be my hammer," Elizabeth said, choosing one.

"That's not fair," Jessica said. "You took the good one."

"I deserve the good one, little sister," Elizabeth said.

"That's right," Steven said. "The oldest should get first pick of everything. I want you to remember that next time Mom makes chocolate cake, Elizabeth. I get the biggest piece."

"Yeah, Elizabeth," Jessica said with a laugh. She picked up a different hammer and started nailing two boards together. "You might be four minutes older than me. But Steven is two whole years older than you."

Just then, Steven jumped up and grabbed the hammer out of Jessica's hand. "Not like that," he said. "You have to use longer nails."

Jessica rolled her eyes, but she picked up a longer nail.

"Now," Steven said. "Let me show you the proper way to hold a hammer."

Jessica sighed.

"Maybe you should make a car of your own, Steven," Elizabeth said.

"Yeah," Jessica agreed. "That way you wouldn't have to boss us around."

Steven pounded in a nail for Jessica. "I already told you, soap-box derbies are for little kids."

"Then maybe Elizabeth's too old to enter," Jessica said sarcastically.

Elizabeth smiled. "I don't blame you for being jealous," she told Jessica. "I'm older and more grown-up than you. Everyone knows it's hard being the youngest."

Jessica didn't say anything. But when Steven handed her hammer back, she pounded in her nails as hard as she could. *Bang! Bang, bang, bang, bang!* Jessica made a lot of noise.

Elizabeth didn't notice that her sister was angry. She was too busy imagining what her car would look like when it was all finished and going at top speed.

CHAPTER 4

Sore Thumbs

The next morning, Jessica was about to walk into the bathroom when Elizabeth slipped in before her.

"You can use the bathroom when I'm finished, little sister," Elizabeth said. She closed the door in Jessica's face.

Jessica stared at the door. Tears gathered in her eyes. Jessica couldn't believe Elizabeth was being so mean to her.

Jessica went down to the kitchen in her

pajamas. "What's for breakfast?" she asked her mother.

"Banana pancakes," Mrs. Wakefield said. She stacked the pancakes from the pan onto a plate on the table.

"Yummy." Jessica sat down. She loved pancakes, especially banana pancakes. She was about to reach for the plate when Elizabeth came into the kitchen.

"Good morning, Mom," Elizabeth said, slipping into a chair. "Aren't you dressed yet, Jessica?"

Jessica stuck out her tongue. "It's Saturday. There's no bus to catch. I can do whatever I want."

Elizabeth shrugged and helped herself to the biggest pancakes with the most bananas. She passed Jessica what was left over.

"May I have the syrup?" Jessica asked, pointing to the half-full bottle.

"Just a second. You can have it when I'm finished," Elizabeth said. She picked up the bottle and tilted it over her pancakes. When she passed the syrup to Jessica, there were only a few drops left in the bottle.

Elizabeth turned to Mrs. Wakefield. "Jessica and I are going to the park right after breakfast."

Jessica stuffed a piece of pancake in her mouth. It didn't taste as good as usual. That was because Elizabeth had ruined breakfast for her. The last thing Jessica wanted to do was go to the park with Elizabeth. But right after breakfast, Jessica got on her bike and rode to the park with her sister anyway. Staying home alone didn't sound like much fun. But Jessica was sick of Elizabeth acting so bossy. She wished their mother had never mentioned that Elizabeth was older.

"Look," Elizabeth said as they neared the park. "Everyone's on the jungle gym. Let's go play with them."

Elizabeth and Jessica parked their bikes and ran toward their friends.

"We started building our cars last night," Elizabeth told everyone. She pulled herself onto the lowest bar of the jungle gym.

Jessica climbed up to the top and sat down. "I pounded in a ton of nails."

Eva was hanging upside down next to her. "Me, too. It sure takes a long time to build these cars. I'm afraid mine will never be finished."

Kisho nodded. "Eva's right. Building a soap-box racer is harder than I thought it would be."

Winston held up his thumb. It was covered with bandages. "I hit my thumb with the hammer—twice."

Everyone laughed.

"It's not funny," Winston said, smiling anyway. "My thumb turned purple. I'm giving up."

"You have to come watch the race, then," Eva said.

"Yeah," Kisho said. "We need fans."

Winston grinned. "Don't worry. I'll be there."

"Do you have any wheels I could use?" Todd asked. "I really need some."

Winston shook his head. "I didn't find any."

"We didn't, either," Elizabeth said.

"I'm not sure what kind to use," Eva said, pulling herself right-side up. "Maybe we should go ask Andy." She pointed to a tree. Andy Franklin was sitting under it, reading

29

a library book. Jessica could see that the book was called *Soap-Box Cars in 10 Easy Steps.*

Jessica hadn't known that Andy was entering the derby. Andy was shy, but he was also very smart. Jessica was sure his car would go fast.

"Hey, Andy," Jessica called out. "We need your help."

Andy looked up. He seemed surprised to hear Jessica calling his name. Most of the time Jessica teased him for being smart.

"What is it?"

"Come over here," Todd said, waving him over.

Andy stood up and walked to the jungle gym. He looked up, squinting into the sun.

"Have you found any wheels?" Todd asked.

"Yeah," Andy said.

"Where?" Elizabeth asked. "We couldn't find any anywhere."

"I got mine off my parents' old lawn mower," Andy said. "But my book says you could also use the wheels from an old baby carriage or a shopping cart."

"I should have thought of that myself," Eva said. "Thanks, Andy!"

"You're welcome," Andy said. He walked back to his spot by the tree.

"Andy's nice," Elizabeth said. "Not like Ken. He's being so secretive."

Eva nodded. "I asked him how his car was going and he wouldn't tell me."

"Maybe we should send Todd to spy on him," Kisho suggested.

"Maybe Ken sent me to spy on you," Todd said, laughing.

"I think Ken is doing his own spying," Jessica said. She pointed across the park. Ken

31

was standing on the sidewalk in front of the park's entrance. A shiny red sports car was parked at the curb. Ken walked around the car, studying it.

Jessica started to feel worried. She climbed down the jungle gym. "Andy," she called. "I want to ask you a favor."

CHAPTER 5

The Junkyard

"Did you find anything?" Jessica asked.

"No," Elizabeth said. She felt discouraged.

It was Sunday and the twins were still trying to find wheels for their soap-box cars. Jessica and Elizabeth were searching the attic for old lawn mowers or baby carriages. But all they found was a lot of dust.

"We're stuck," Jessica said. "There's nothing here. What are we going to do?"

"The same thing we always do when we're stuck," Elizabeth said. "Ask Mom."

Mrs. Wakefield was sitting in the living room, working on her interior-design homework. When the twins explained their problem, she thought for a moment. "How about going to the junkyard tomorrow?" she suggested. "I bet we'll find all kinds of wheels there."

"Junkyard?" Jessica asked, wrinkling her nose. "That sounds dirty."

"It's that or no wheels," Elizabeth said. "Trust your big sister."

Jessica sighed. "All right."

The next day after school, the twins and Steven piled into the car. Mrs. Wakefield drove past the mall, the supermarket, and the movie theater, and kept on going. After a while, the houses started to get farther and farther apart. Finally, Mrs. Wakefield

34

turned into a narrow gravel driveway that led to a winding country road.

"Here we are," she announced. "The search is about to begin."

The junkyard was surrounded by a wooden fence. Mrs. Wakefield rang a bell at the gate. A woman in brown overalls let them in. "Welcome, welcome," she said. "Happy hunting."

A large, black dog barked as the Wakefields came in. Jessica took her mother's hand, but she let go when she saw that the dog was wagging its tail.

"There's so much stuff here," Jessica said, looking around at the mountain of junk. There were old engines, chairs without seats, kitchen sinks, rusty bicycles without wheels, cracked pots, and lots of other things no one had any more use for.

35

"This place is great," Steven said. He ran over to an old empty soda machine.

Jessica, Elizabeth, and Mrs. Wakefield began to wander around, too. They walked from pile to pile of junk, finding several wheels that were much too small for their derby cars.

Then Elizabeth and Jessica both spotted the same pair of wheels. "Look," they said at exactly the same time.

"Those are perfect," Jessica shouted.

"They are," Elizabeth agreed. She put her arms around the wheels. They were big and fat, with heavy treads. "These are mine, little sister."

"No fair," Jessica yelled, trying to yank the wheels out of Elizabeth's arms.

Elizabeth kept a firm grip. "You can be such a baby sometimes, Jessica."

"Elizabeth," Mrs. Wakefield said, coming

36

up behind them. "That's not a very nice thing to say. It's not like you to be so thoughtless. I want you to apologize."

Elizabeth frowned. "Sorry, Jess," she whispered. But she didn't really mean it.

"I'll help you find some more wheels," Steven told Jessica.

"Thanks." Jessica followed him.

Elizabeth didn't help them. She just sat on a broken chair in the shade and watched. She saw Steven find pair after pair of wheels, but Jessica didn't like any of them. They were all too small. Jessica refused to leave until they found some that she liked.

"I want wheels just like the ones Elizabeth has," Jessica said loudly. "Heavy wheels will make the car go faster."

Andy had shown Jessica his library book at the park on Saturday. She had read all about wheels and axles and steering.

"No way," Steven said. "Lighter cars go faster."

"Want to bet?" Jessica asked.

"OK," Steven said. "But if I'm right, you have to do my chores for a week."

"And if *I'm* right, you have to help me build my soap-box car," Jessica said.

Steven nodded. "It's a deal."

They shook hands.

Elizabeth didn't care who won the bet. She just wanted to go home and put her wheels on her car. "Hurry up," she shouted to Jessica.

Jessica didn't look at her. Instead she ran over to Mrs. Wakefield, who was heading back from another part of the junkyard. "Mom, we need to ask you something."

"Yeah. Will Jessica's car go faster if it has heavy wheels or light ones?" Steven asked.

Mrs. Wakefield thought for a moment.

"Light cars with engines go faster," she said. "But since soap-box cars don't have engines, they would pick up more speed if they're heavy, so the answer is heavy wheels."

Steven's mouth fell open.

"I win," Jessica said, smiling and poking Steven. "Now let's find some heavy wheels."

Elizabeth bit her lip. "Are you sure?" she asked her mother, once Jessica and Steven were out of earshot.

"Absolutely," Mrs. Wakefield said.

Elizabeth looked down at the wheels resting on her lap. The fact that she had chosen heavy wheels was an accident. *I didn't know that the weight of the car was important,* she thought. And she couldn't believe her little sister knew something she didn't.

CHAPTER 6
Sore Winner

On the bus ride home from school the next day, Caroline told Elizabeth and Jessica all about everyone's cars. Todd had put a bicycle seat in his. Andy had used metal from the body of a real car. Eva had decided to use a pizza pan for a steering wheel. The only person who hadn't told Caroline anything was Ken. "He's hiding something," Caroline said. "I just know it."

"Maybe he wants to surprise us on Saturday," Elizabeth said. "He probably did something fancy, like put signal lights on the back."

Jessica grinned. "Or maybe his car is a mess and he's embarrassed."

Caroline shook her head. "I don't think so. Remember what Ken said about his dad?"

"Caroline's right," Elizabeth said. "His car will be great."

Jessica shrugged. She didn't care that Ken's dad had been a champion. She was still sure she could win.

When the twins got off the bus, Jessica skipped ahead to catch up with Steven. "Don't forget you have to help me with my car this afternoon," she told him.

"I didn't forget," Steven said. "But I need energy. How about giving me your snack?"

"No way," Jessica said. "The driver needs to eat more."

Jessica rushed inside their house and

drank her milk and ate her piece of cake in record time.

"Come on, we have work to do," she said, jumping up from the kitchen table and pulling Steven by the arms so hard that he almost choked on his milk.

"OK. Hold your horses. I'm coming."

Jessica dragged Steven out into the garage while Elizabeth stayed to finish her snack.

"The body is almost finished," Jessica said, pointing to her car. She opened a lawn chair and sat down. "You should attach the wheels now."

Steven raised his eyebrows. "I'm supposed to be *helping* you, not taking orders like your personal slave."

"I'll help later," Jessica answered. "Right now, get to work."

"Jess-ic-a," Steven said, clearly annoyed.

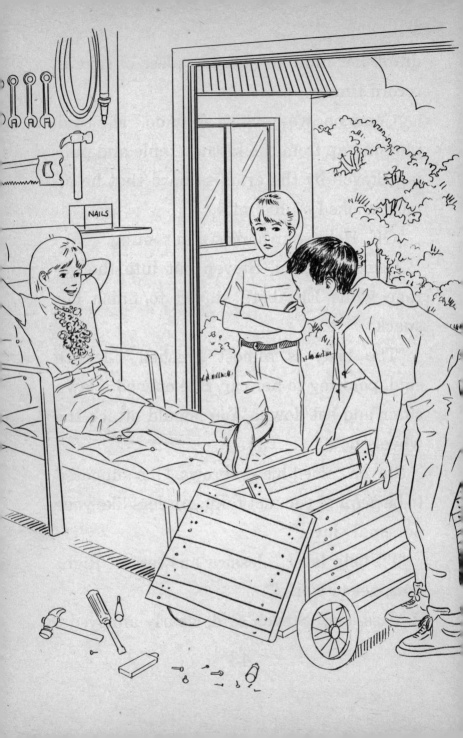

"Please," Jessica pleaded.

Steven sighed. "We've got to screw the body together tighter," he said. "See how solid Elizabeth's car is?" He went over to the other car and shook the sides. The wood didn't budge. "You want yours to be like hers."

Jessica crossed her arms in front of her chest. "For your information, I do *not* want my car to be like Elizabeth's. So stop trying to tell me what to do."

"Steven just wants to help you," Elizabeth said as she came in to the garage. "You should listen. He *is* older than you are, you know."

"He's older than you, too," Jessica yelled. "And you don't let him tell you what to do. So stop bossing me around. I'm sick of it. And I'm sick of you!"

Elizabeth's face turned red. "Shut up," she yelled back.

"I will not. It used to be fun having a twin sister," Jessica went on. "But it isn't anymore—it's a big pain!"

Elizabeth didn't say anything. Instead, she concentrated on screwing a screw into her car.

"Fine," Jessica said. "Don't talk to me. See if I care."

Elizabeth didn't talk to Jessica for the rest of the afternoon or all that night. That was fine with Jessica. She was still mad when she went to bed.

During recess the following morning, Jessica played with Lila and Ellen. Elizabeth played with Todd and Eva.

"Are you and Elizabeth having a fight?" Ellen asked Jessica.

"Yes," Jessica said. "Elizabeth's been acting like a jerk since Mom told her she was older than me. I'm not going to talk to her until she tells me she's sorry."

But Elizabeth didn't apologize to Jessica all that day. She didn't apologize at home that evening, either. Elizabeth didn't even say good night to Jessica at bedtime. By then, Jessica was beginning to wish Elizabeth would hurry up and say she was sorry. Jessica was getting lonely.

CHAPTER 7
The Route

"Are you OK?" Amy asked Elizabeth on Thursday morning. "You seem sad."

Elizabeth looked down at her sneakers. "Jessica and I still aren't speaking."

"Wow," Amy said. "It's been two whole days, hasn't it?"

Elizabeth nodded.

"Take your seats, everyone," Mrs. Otis called out. "I have an important announcement to make."

Elizabeth guessed that Mrs. Otis was going to tell them something about the derby. Everyone else must have guessed the same thing, because the room got quiet in record time.

Mrs. Otis smiled. "I have the route for the derby," she began. "It's marked in red on this map of Secca Lake." She passed out photocopies of the map to each student. The route started at the top of a steep hill and went all the way down, and ran across a long straightaway.

"To make it over the finish line, you're going to have to build up a lot of speed coming down that hill," Mrs. Otis told the class.

"No problem," Todd called out. "It's going to be just like a roller coaster."

The race was only two days away. Everyone was excited. Even Elizabeth had a hard time concentrating on her math problems.

During recess, all anyone talked about was the derby.

"My car is finished," Jessica told Ken.

"Mine, too," Ken boasted. "It's been finished for two days now. I already tried it out on Mulberry Street."

Elizabeth, Amy, Eva, Todd, Lila, and Ellen gathered around.

"Wow," Eva said. "That street is steep."

"Really steep," Ken agreed. He smiled proudly. "My car flew."

"Are you going to try it out again?" Todd asked.

Ken nodded. "You bet. I'm going to spend every afternoon until the race practicing. Only now I can practice at Secca Lake on the real course."

"I'll be there, too," Eva said.

Jessica stepped forward. "I got two great pairs of wheels," she told Ken. "They might have come off a truck." She threw her arms open as wide as she could. "They're this big."

"They're not better than mine," Ken said. "My dad told me—"

"That's another thing," Jessica interrupted. "I built my car all by myself. I didn't have to have my father help me."

Ken ignored Jessica. He looked at everyone gathered around. "My dad told me," he continued in a loud voice, "that my soap-box derby car is the best one he's ever seen. He says it's even better than the one he won in."

"Who cares what your dad says?" Elizabeth said. "My car is super sturdy. Right, Jess?" She looked at her sister for the first time since they stopped speaking. "And *I* really did build it all on my own."

She looked at Jessica again, then at Ken. "See you at Secca Lake."

CHAPTER 8
Practice Runs

"Mom," Jessica called, running into the living room. The twins had run all the way home from the bus stop that afternoon. "Can we take the cars to Secca Lake?"

"We need to practice for Saturday," Elizabeth said.

"Everyone's going," Jessica added.

Mrs. Wakefield put down her newspaper and smiled. "Well, if everyone's going, how could I say no?"

"Are you going to come?" Elizabeth asked Steven.

"No," Steven said. "I'm going over to Joe's. But let me know how *my* car does."

Jessica stuck out her tongue. "You only *wish* it were your car."

Mrs. Wakefield and the twins loaded both cars into the van. When they reached Secca Lake, most of the twins' friends were already there. Kisho, Todd, Eva, and Amy Sutton were examining each other's cars. Lila, Ellen, and Winston were there to watch.

Lila ran up to the Wakefields' car as soon as it stopped.

Jessica jumped out. "Hi, Lila! Is Ken here yet?"

"No, but look," Lila said, pointing down the hill. "The finish line has already been painted."

Jessica saw the bright white line way

down at the bottom of the hill. Her heart started beating faster. She couldn't wait to try out her car.

"Everyone's taking turns on the hill," Lila went on. "It looks scary."

Mrs. Wakefield helped unload the cars. Then Elizabeth and Jessica watched as Todd jumped into his car. Kisho gave the car a big push, and Todd rolled down the hill.

"Go, go," Ellen and Lila cheered.

"Faster!" Winston yelled. "Faster."

But Todd's car rolled slowly. It couldn't go very fast because its wheels were loose. Everyone giggled.

Todd was laughing, too, as he and Winston pushed his car back up the hill. "I guess I have some last-minute adjustments to make."

When it was her turn, Jessica strapped on her helmet, jumped in her car, and flew down the hill. The wind blew in her face. Jessica never touched the brakes. She loved going fast.

"That was super, super fun," Jessica said as Mrs. Wakefield helped her push the car back up for another run. "I can't wait for it to be my turn again."

Next, Kisho and Todd gave Elizabeth a push. When her car started to go fast, Elizabeth hit the brakes. She slowed to a stop at the very bottom of the hill.

"That was scary," Elizabeth said as Mrs. Wakefield helped her push her car back up for another run.

"You need more speed," Todd called out.

"Next time," Elizabeth called back. "That was just a warm-up."

Soon, Jessica was flying down the hill again. She was going even faster than she had the first time. Then suddenly—BANG!

One side of her car fell off! BANG! Then the other side. By the time Jessica rolled across the finish line, her car had completely fallen apart. Pieces of it were scattered down the hill.

"Are you OK?" Mrs. Wakefield asked, rushing over. "You had my heart beating doubletime."

"I'm fine," Jessica said. She wasn't hurt, but she was disappointed. Without a car, she wouldn't be able to race.

"See?" Elizabeth said, when Jessica got back to the top of the hill. "You should have listened to Steven and made your car like mine."

"Maybe yours will fall apart, too," Jessica shot back. "Just try going as fast I did, slow-poke."

Elizabeth didn't answer. She simply stomped off and tried again, and again, and again to drive down the hill with more speed. Todd and Eva cheered her on. But Elizabeth slowed to a complete stop long before she came close to the finish line.

Jessica watched and knew that Elizabeth must be scared to go fast. *Now Liz can't act superior,* she thought. *Maybe she'll forget she's four stupid minutes older.*

CHAPTER 9
Ken's Car

Ken finally arrived at Secca Lake. He and his mother unloaded his car. It was beautiful. While the other cars were made of ordinary wood and metal and plastic, Ken's was made of wood, but painted bright red.

Everyone gathered around.

"Wow," Eva said. "Red is a real sports-car color."

Ken patted the car. "Isn't it perfect?"

Winston nodded. "You did a really good job."

"I know," Ken said.

"Are the wheels on tight?" Todd asked with a smile.

Ken gave Todd a weird look. "Of course."

"Do you want to take a turn on the hill?" Kisho asked.

Ken yawned. "There's no hurry. You guys go ahead. You need the practice more than I do."

He looked around and walked over to where Jessica was sitting with Ellen and Lila. "Where's your car, Jessica?"

Jessica's face turned red. "It's broken," she whispered.

"You should have been here, Ken," Todd said. "It was wild. Jessica's car broke into about a hundred pieces on the second run."

Ken laughed. "I knew a sissy girl would never beat me," he said.

Elizabeth was standing nearby, and she overheard what Ken said. She was furious. Though she was mad at Jessica, she didn't like having her sister made fun of. For the first time, Elizabeth wanted not just to race—she wanted to beat Ken. But Elizabeth knew she didn't have the nerve. She might dream of going fast, but speed scared her.

"Let's go home," Elizabeth told her mom. "I don't want to practice anymore."

"Are you ready to go, Jessica?" Mrs. Wakefield asked.

Jessica nodded. "If I only had a car," she said, her eyes focused on Ken. "I'd show him."

On the way home, Elizabeth thought

hard. She didn't want Ken to win. But how could she stop him?

Suddenly, Elizabeth had an idea. A brilliant idea. She turned to Jessica and smiled. "I need your help."

CHAPTER 10
Victory!

Tons of people were milling around Secca Lake on Saturday morning, the day of the big race. There was even a photographer from the *Sweet Valley News*.

The Wakefields started to push Elizabeth's car up to the starting line. Lila and Ellen and Winston ran up to help.

"How do you feel?" Jessica asked Elizabeth.

"My tummy is turning somersaults," Elizabeth answered.

"Mine, too," Jessica said.

Ken was already at the starting line with his dad. Mr. Matthews was studying the other kids' cars, and whispering instructions to Ken.

All of the second graders would be in a qualifying heat. Then the six fastest cars would race again for first, second, and third place.

"Get ready, kids," yelled an official, who was carrying a flag.

Jessica climbed into Elizabeth's car.

"Hey, what are you doing?" Lila shouted. "That's not yours."

"I know," Jessica said calmly.

"How come you're letting your *little sister* drive your car?" Ellen asked Elizabeth.

"I'm a little older than Jessica," Elizabeth said, "but Jessica does some things better than I do."

Jessica smiled as she fastened her helmet.

"Go get him," Elizabeth said, slapping Jessica on the back.

The cars lined up. The official waved the flag in the air and then snapped it down in front of the starting line.

It happened so fast that Elizabeth and Steven were taken by surprise. By the time they gave Jessica her push, the other cars had a head start. Jessica rolled down the hill fast, but she had lost too much distance to catch up to the front runners. She came in sixth. Ken came in first.

"Jessica and Ken both made the finals," Steven said.

"So did Todd, Andy, Eva, and Amy," Elizabeth added. "This is great."

Steven and Elizabeth ran down the hill and helped Jessica push Elizabeth's car back up. Ken's father was helping Ken push his car.

"See?" Ken yelled to Jessica. "I told you I'd beat you."

"You haven't beaten me yet," Jessica yelled back. "That was just a trial run. Wait until the real race."

"OK then, good luck in the real race," Ken said with a smirk. "You'll need it." Mr. Matthews laughed and slapped Ken on the back.

At the top of the hill, Jessica climbed back into the car. She took a deep breath.

"Don't be nervous," Elizabeth whispered. "Just race like you did the other day." Jessica nodded.

This time when the flag came down, Steven and Elizabeth were ready. They pushed Jessica as hard as they could. Jessica got off to a great start, but Ken and Todd still were ahead of her.

"Go, Jess!" Elizabeth yelled. "You can do it."

Jessica heard the shouts of encouragement. She held on tight to her steering wheel and kept the car steady.

Then about halfway down the hill, one of Todd's wheels rolled off! His car turned sideways and stopped. Jessica was headed right for him.

"She's going to crash," Steven yelled. "Watch out, Jessica!"

But at the last second, Jessica steered around Todd's car. She missed him by an inch.

"All right!" Elizabeth yelled. "Keep going."

Jessica was picking up speed. She saw Ken. Now more than ever she wanted to take home the trophy. She leaned forward in the car to go even faster. It worked. A second later Jessica and Ken were lined up hood and hood. Andy was close behind. "Go, Jessica," Steven screamed.

Jessica pulled ahead.

Elizabeth jumped up and down. "Jessica! Jessica! Jessica!"

Seconds later, Jessica zipped across the finish line—in first place!

Andy came in second. Ken finished third.

Elizabeth ran down the hill. She wasn't afraid of going fast on her own two feet.

Jessica took off her helmet. She was grinning. "How was that?"

"Awesome," Elizabeth shouted, giving her a tight hug.

Cameras flashed all around them. "Nice race," Ken said, walking up to them. "But wait until next year."

Jessica grinned some more. "Thanks. I couldn't have done it without my *big* sister's help."

Mr. and Mrs. Wakefield and Steven ran over.

"Congratulations!" Mr. Wakefield said. "You're a born driver."

"Yeah, not bad," Steven said. "You squirts did a good job."

"Between Elizabeth's car and Jessica's driving," Mrs. Wakefield said, "I'd say you're both champions."

"If we're champions," Jessica said, "then do we get to celebrate?"

Mrs. Wakefield's eyes twinkled. "What do you have in mind?"

"I'd like to go to the beach tomorrow," Jessica answered.

"Good idea," Elizabeth agreed. "We could have a picnic."

Mrs. Wakefield smiled. "That is a good idea."

"I'll pack an extra-special victory lunch," Mr. Wakefield said.

Eva ran up to them. Her parents were close behind. "I came in fourth!" Eva yelled.

"Another champion," Mrs. Wakefield said, winking at Mrs. Simpson.

"Eva and her parents should come to the beach with us tomorrow," Elizabeth said.

"The beach?" Mrs. Simpson asked.

"We're going to celebrate there," Jessica explained.

"That's sure to be fun," Mrs. Simpson said. "Want to go?" she asked Eva and Mr. Simpson.

Eva jumped up and down. "Yes!"

Mr. Simpson smiled. "Sounds good to me. I can't remember the last time I dipped my feet in the ocean."

"Is work keeping you busy?" Mr. Wakefield asked.

"I'll say," Mr. Simpson answered with a sigh. "And to think I used to go to the beach almost every day when we lived in Jamaica. I really miss the beaches of my island home."

"The beaches here are nice, too," Eva said. "We're going to have a terrific time!"

Could anything spoil the twins' victory celebration at the beach? Find out in Sweet Valley Kids #38, GOOD-BYE, EVA?